MB 15·9·12

Also by Jon Mayhew:

Mortlock

The Demon Collector

The Bonehill Curse

DEATHMIRE

JON MAYHEW

LONDON·SYDNEY

First published in 2012
by Franklin Watts

Text © Jon Mayhew 2012
Cover design by Cathryn Gilbert

Franklin Watts
338 Euston Road
London NW1 3BH

Franklin Watts Australia
Level 17/207 Kent Street
Sydney, NSW 2000

A CIP catalogue record for this book
is available from the British Library.

Slava Gerj/Shutterstock: front cover c.
Anna Kucherova/Shutterstock: front cover b.
lolloj/Shutterstock: front cover top.

ISBN: 978 1 4451 1466 8

1 3 5 7 9 10 8 6 4 2

Printed in Great Britain

Franklin Watts is a division of
Hachette Children's Books,
an Hachette UK company.
www.hachette.co.uk

To Frank, Ben, James and Craig

Contents

Chapter One

It was a scream of horror, Tom Striker knew that straight away. He'd heard people scream when they'd stepped in front of a horse and carriage, or slipped on wet cobbles. That kind of scream tended to be short, and more to do with the sudden surprise. The scream he'd just heard was prolonged and made his skin prickle into gooseflesh. But worse than that, Tom knew it was the voice of Billy Simpkins.

Not even half an hour earlier, he and Billy had agreed to split up so that they weren't sifting through the same river mud. They were looking for anything worth money: coins; lost watches; scraps of metal; rags; bones; even teeth sometimes, although they often came attached to a smeared and bleached skull.

"You go by the water's edge, Billy," Tom had said.

"What? You scared of the river?" Billy jeered at him.

Tom had just scowled and stalked off. Billy knew he was scared of water. Tom couldn't swim a stroke to save his life. He had nearly drowned once after falling in the river.

Billy had vanished into the thickening mist, bent over and squelching towards the river's edge, while Tom inched along nearer the river wall. Tom didn't find much: an old belt without a buckle, made stiff by the water.

And then Billy had screamed.

Tom ran through the mist, slithering and sliding towards the water's edge. The river lapped innocently against the grey mud. There was no sight or sound of Billy himself. No splashing. No shouting. Then Tom saw Billy's flat cap floating on the black Thames, just in front of him.

He reached out for it.

"What happened?" An urgent voice cried out, making Tom twist round and almost fall flat in the mud.

"Oh, it's only you," Tom gasped. Ophelia stood there shivering. She'd joined them a few weeks ago, scavenging in the mud. Not many girls went mudlarking, but she'd proved herself to be good at navigating the deeper, more treacherous mudflows. That's where you could get stuck up to your thighs. If that happened you would have to wait for a passing longshoreman to rescue you, before the river rose up and drowned you.

"Where's Billy?" The fear in Ophelia's voice infected Tom, making his heart beat faster.

"I don't know," Tom said. "I heard him scream. All I can see is his hat."

"He must have fallen in," Ophelia whispered. She lurched

away from the water, the mud
squelching and sucking at her
legs as she did. "Or maybe he
was dragged in by a whale or
something."

"A whale?" Tom sneered, trying
to sound brave. "Don't be daft!"
Did such huge sea monsters swim
upriver? He didn't really know.

"We should get the others,
quick!" Ophelia said, gripping
Tom's arm and making him wince.
Tom glanced at her. Her thin grey
dress clung to her skinny frame,

her lank wet hair stuck to her pale face. She looked like she hadn't eaten in days but that grip was strong. "They'll help find him."

Together, they slithered and slipped across the mud back to the stone steps as quickly as they could. Tom glanced back through the mist, but nothing broke the inky black water's surface.

Chapter Two

Ophelia stopped when they got
to the top of the stone steps.

"I'll wait here," she declared.
"In case Billy turns up. You never
know, he might've been playing
a prank."

"Suit yourself," Tom sniffed.
He turned on his heel and stalked
off to find Herbert and Wilf. They
were mudlarks too, but a bit
older. They might know what to
do about Billy.

The alleyways narrowed and the
courtyards Tom passed through
became filthier, more littered
with rubbish. The darkness
thickened and fog crept up from
the river, filling every street.

A cry for help gave Tom a start.

"What now?" Tom muttered, his nerves already rattled. The sound was close, but in the gloom he could only make out a group of grey figures.

"Give us all your money," said a nasal voice from one of the figures.

"Come on, we ain't got all day," said another voice.

"I don't have no money," croaked the weak voice of the victim. "Please, leave me alone."

"No funny business, now, or I'll stick you with me knife," snarled the first voice.

It was a robbery! The two shadowy figures had set upon an old man. Tom felt his anger blaze.

"Oi!" Tom shouted from the shadows, deepening his voice and trying his best to sound like a police constable. "Leave the old feller alone!"

"Lookout, it's a copper," one of the robbers gasped. That made Tom smirk.

"Quick, run for it!" the other yelled back.

Tom smiled, satisfied at the clatter of footsteps as the two robbers ran off into the thick fog.

He walked over cautiously to a bulky figure lying on the ground. Deep lines wrinkled the man's ancient face. He wore several different ragged coats, making Tom wonder if he was really as big as he looked under all the clothes. The old fellow groaned.

"You all right, mister?" Tom whispered, squatting down.

"I'll be fine," the man croaked. "Just give me a minute. Young rapscallions. If they knew who they were threatening, then they wouldn't have been so sure of themselves..."

"Wouldn't they?" Tom said, frowning as the old man dragged himself to his feet with a wince.

"Not if they knew that I was

Old Father Thames, himself,"
the old man declared, holding
his head up.

Chapter Three

"So, you're Old Father Thames..."
Tom said, taking a step back
from the old man. Now he was
back on his feet he towered over
the boy. I haven't got time for
this, Tom thought, I've got to
find Wilf and Herbert.

"Oh, I know you won't believe me, boy," the old man muttered, shaking his head. "It's true, though. I'm the spirit of these waters. An' I have been for more years than what I can remember."

"Of course you have." Tom rolled his eyes. Trust my luck to rescue a barm pot! he thought.

With surprising speed, the old man grabbed Tom's sleeve and clamped his grimy hand around the boy's wrist. "But Old Jenny Greenteeth stole me crown," the old man hissed, wide-eyed. Tom tried to pull away, but the man had a grip like a pincer. "She'll fill the river with her minions. Mark my words."

"Let go," Tom yelled. "You're hurting me wrist!"

The old man gazed down at his hand as if it belonged to someone else. Then he eased his hold, allowing Tom to stagger back.

"I'm sorry," the old man said as Tom backed away. "Don't fear the water, son. Fear what's in it. Grab her crown if you can."

But Tom only heard the words shouted in the distance. He was already hurrying down the street, away from the mad old man.

Tom finally found Wilf and Herbert outside a gin shop, begging coins from the drunkards that staggered out.

"It don't sound too good for Billy," Wilf declared after Tom finished his story of the last hour.

"Let's go and have a look-see," Herbert suggested.

Tom hurried after the two boys as they plunged into the misty streets. The stink of the River Thames quickly filled Tom's nostrils again. His stomach fluttered a little. What was it Ophelia had said? A sea monster had dragged Billy in?

Ophelia stood on the shore, twisting the hem of her grey, stained apron in her hands. The river looked eerie in its veil of

fog, and the last daylight faded as
night drew in.

"You took your time, Tom,"
she snapped. "Poor Billy could be
washed out to sea by now."

"Well, you better shut up
and help us search then," Tom
muttered, trying to sound brave.

"Don't worry, Ophelia," Herbert
growled, puffing out his chest.
"You can come with me. I'll
protect you."

Tom rolled his eyes and gave
Wilf a nod to follow him.

The water lapped listlessly at
the muddy shore as Tom squelched
along its edge.

"It's impossible to see in this,"
he groaned to Wilf, who peered
out into the fog. "An' it'll be pitch
dark soon."

"Yeah," Wilf agreed, kicking
at a rotten beam that poked out
from the grey slime.

A sudden scream from behind them smothered Tom's reply.

"That was Herbert!" Wilf hissed, turning and skating across the mud. Tom chased after him in a slithering run. His heart pounded and he felt as if he would never get to where the screams and splashes were coming from.

Wilf stopped short so quickly that Tom skidded into him.

"Oh, Lord," Wilf whispered, staring at a sight that had

paralysed him. Tom peered over his shoulder at the most hideous scene he had ever encountered.

Chapter Four

Tom stood, as helpless as Wilf, staring at the couple in the water.

Herbert was up to his waist in the filthy Thames, wrestling with Billy!

Only it wasn't Billy.

It looked like him but the skin was grey and dead. Billy's eyes glowed bulbous and black, much too big for his face. And his mouth curved in an upside-down grin full of green, needle teeth. He looked more fish than human, more dead than alive.

Herbert sobbed with terror, desperately trying to wade to shore and push Billy away at the same time.

"Help me," Herbert panted. Then with a cry, he fell back into the water. The creature plunged after him with a hiss. The water frothed and bubbled as the two sank from sight, then all was still.

Tom looked at Wilf. The sound of someone scurrying across the muddy shoreline made them turn. It was Ophelia. She was pale and panting.

"Did you see?" she gasped. "Did you see it?"

"Where were you?" Tom snarled, turning his anger and sorrow on the girl, rather than trying to understand what he'd just seen. "You could've saved him!"

"I was just further up the shore," Ophelia said, frowning. "It weren't my fault. What could I have done? That...that thing was hideous!"

"He didn't stand a chance," Wilf whispered, his face drawn and white.

Tom looked down at his own trembling hands as he remembered the parting words of the old man.

"Old Jenny Greenteeth stole my crown. She'll fill the river with her minions," he'd said.

Billy's teeth had been green, like rusty copper nails.

"I reckon we look for this old man I saw," Tom said, gently pulling at Wilf's sleeve. "He said he was Old Father Thames..."

"That old fool?" Ophelia spat. She glowered at Tom. "What will he know? He's barmy!"

"Well, what then?" Tom felt his anger rising. "I've never seen nothing like that before. It ain't natural. You can sit an' wait for Billy to come back, but I'm going to find the old man. Come on, Wilf."

Tom dragged Wilf away and headed off to find Old Father Thames. Ophelia stood, arms folded, on the cold shore.

As it turned out, the old man wasn't far away. He was huddled by a driftwood fire at the foot of some stone steps.

"So you believe me now?" he called as Tom and Wilf approached.

"I dunno what to believe," Tom replied.

"Jenny Greenteeth must be stopped," Old Father Thames croaked. The glow of the flames deepened the wrinkles in his face, making him look even more ancient.

"But who, or what, is she?" Wilf whispered.

"A water spirit like me self. Evil

though. Delights in dragging souls to the depths. Changing them, making them like her," Old Father Thames said. "As folks flock into the city, they bring their superstitions and beliefs with them. Someone brought Jenny Greenteeth."

"If you're who you say you are, why can't you stop her?" Tom retorted.

Old Father Thames heaved a deep sigh and pulled his ragged coat around him. "I'm old," he groaned. "I'm the spirit of the waters. They are polluted, and I am weak. Only something as foul as Greenteeth could flourish in such a place. Besides, she has stolen me crown. Without it, I'm nothing."

"Right then, we'll stay away from the river," Tom muttered, glancing at Wilf, who nodded in agreement.

"But she must be stopped," Old Father Thames repeated. "Otherwise she'll keep dragging people into the river, changing them like she changed your friend. It'll never stop until every last person is gone."

"But if you can't stop her," Wilf squeaked, "how will we?"

"Your friend is brave," Old Father Thames said, lifting his head and piercing Tom with his haunting eyes. "He has a good heart."

"Yeah an' he's terrified of water," Wilf said.

"You have to be cunning. She is full of pride and cannot resist a challenge," Old Father Thames said. "If you can tempt her onto dry land, hold her there and tear the crown from her head, she will be defenceless. Give me the crown, I can do the rest."

Tom looked at Wilf and then glanced over his shoulder at the murky reflections on the night water. He thought about Billy's twisted face and Herbert's last plea for help.

"All right then," he murmured. "I'll give it a go."

Chapter Five

Old Father Thames had made it sound so simple, but now Tom stood on the pier at Miller's Wharf, he wasn't so sure.

"So you're going to call this spirit, and then what?" Ophelia snorted. She'd caught up with them as they left the old man and headed for the wharf.

"You'll see," Tom muttered. Something bothered him and he couldn't quite work it out. It was like a piece of a jigsaw that hadn't quite found a place.

"Oi! Jenny Greenteeth!" he shouted into the night. He felt stupid. Shouting at a phantom from some mad old man's imagination. But then he had seen Billy. He hadn't imagined that.

"You're all very brave skulking in the river. Why don't you come up here on the pier an' talk to us? You afraid?"

Silence.

He could feel Ophelia's scornful gaze at his back. And a piece of the jigsaw snapped into place.

"Try again, Tom," Wilf said in a faint voice.

"Nah," Tom muttered. "I reckon I don't need to shout. She can hear me plain as day."

"What d'you mean?" Wilf whimpered.

"Maybe Ophelia can explain," Tom said, turning on the girl.

"How did you guess?" Ophelia said, grinning unpleasantly.

"You were there just after Billy went," Tom said, narrowing his eyes. "And when Herbert died..."

"So were you," Ophelia sneered.

"Yeah, but then before, when I mentioned the old man," Tom countered, "you spoke as if you knew him. You called him 'that old fool'. You've been leading me on. Getting me to bring me friends down here so you could kill them."

"Not kill," Ophelia said, her grin widening, her jaw stretching with needle teeth, her eyes bulging into reflective globes as she transformed into Jenny Greenteeth. "They're still here, just changed."

She lunged at Wilf and gave him a shove. With a shriek, Wilf stumbled to the edge of the pier and tumbled down into the grey mud below.

Tom leapt at Jenny Greenteeth, head-butting her and sending her sprawling to the ground. She mustn't get to the water, he thought. As long as she's on dry land, she's weak.

"You enjoyed fooling us," Tom snarled, swinging a punch.

"It's always a risk coming ashore," Jenny hissed, lashing out with blackened talons. "But it was such fun watching you bring new victims to me so eagerly."

Tom threw himself at her and pinned her arms to her sides. He could see the crown's dull gleam in her lank hair. He tried to grab at it, but Jenny launched forward and he found himself on the edge of the pier, still clinging to her. All it would take was one simple roll and they would both fall into the water.

But Jenny Greenteeth twisted until she pinned Tom with her body. Tom glimpsed Wilf staggering about in the mud below. But two shapes began to emerge from beneath the black surface of the water. Tom recognised Billy straight away, grinning and hissing. Beside him, changed now, stood Herbert. He leered at Wilf as the poor boy floundered in the mire.

"Soon you will join him as one of my servants," Jenny Greenteeth cackled. "I've a soft spot for you, Tom. I might make you my special slave!"

A hot surge of anger burst up from Tom's stomach. She had done this. She had taken his friends away, made them inhuman. With a roar, Tom punched out, catching Jenny Greenteeth right on her pointed chin. The creature fell back and Tom pounced on her, clawing at her eyes, pulling at her hair.

Blow by blow he drove her back up the pier, away from the water.

Old Father Thames loomed from behind a pile of crates.

"The crown," he cried. "Grab the crown!"

With a final yell of defiance, Tom ripped the metal band from around Jenny Greenteeth's head and threw it to Old Father Thames.

Only Jenny Greenteeth's furious shrieks broke the silence as the old man placed the crown on his head. He grew in stature, his beard was cleaner, his eyes glowed with a light that Tom hadn't seen in them before.

Old Father Thames strode over to Jenny Greenteeth and pulled her to her feet.

"Now child," he said gruffly. "No more games." He turned to Tom. "Thank you, boy. You have a stout heart. I am in your debt. If ever you should need me, just call to the River. Your friends are safe. I will deal with this one myself."

He dragged Jenny Greenteeth by the wrist. She turned to give Tom one last baleful glare, and then she and Old Father Thames plunged off the end of the pier into the black depths below.

Wilf dragged himself back up onto the pier. "'As she g-g-gone?" he gasped.

"Yeah," said Tom. "But what about Billy an' Herbert?"

"Down there," Wilf nodded over his shoulder.

Tom ran to the pier's edge and stared down at his two dazed friends. They stood, knee-deep in mud, shaking their heads.

"They're back to normal," Tom laughed. He looked thoughtfully across the river. "An' I don't ever have to fear the water again."

About the author

Jon Mayhew is the award-winning author of *Mortlock*, *The Demon Collector* and *The Bonehill Curse*. Victorian London has always fascinated him and he loves spooky stories. Jon grew up by the banks of the River Mersey, another smelly and foggy river. He considers growing a beard every two months but never does. If he was a Victorian gentleman, he certainly would.

You can find out more about Jon's books at:

www.jonmayhew.co.uk

PAYBACK

GRAHAM MARKS

EDGE

If you enjoyed reading
DEATHMIRE, you might also like
PAYBACK, by Graham Marks.

There's a voice in his head, and everywhere
Greg looks someone is ready to die...

You know when you do something that
you instantly regret? Well that's how it
starts for Greg. In the park, he sees it lying
there: a smooth, black oblong of glass.

www.marksworks.co.uk

Buy online at
www.franklinwatts.co.uk
978 1 4451 1442 2 paperback
978 1 4451 1443 9 eBook

**Turn over to read an extract from
PAYBACK:**

"Hello," said a voice. "Good to meet you, Gregory..."

Greg jumped up, like he'd been stung by a wasp, and glanced behind him. But there was no one there.

"Who?" he frowned. "Where?"

"You called," said the voice.

Greg froze. The voice was coming from the-thing-that-wasn't-a-phone which he was still holding. He looked down

at it to find that the black glass
surface now looked like there
was a drawing of an old-fashioned
scythe etched into it.

"Not me...I didn't call anyone,"
Greg said. "Who are you — and
how do you know my name?"

"I do apologise, how rude of me!
I'm Michael, but as we are going
to be working together, you can
call me Mike."

**To find out who Mike is and how he's going to work
with Greg, get hold of a copy of Payback today!**

Also available from EDGE.
CRIME TEAM adventures by The 2Steves,
where YOU crack the case!

978 0 7496 9283 4 pb
978 1 4451 0843 8 eBook

978 0 7496 9284 1 pb
978 1 4451 0844 5 eBook

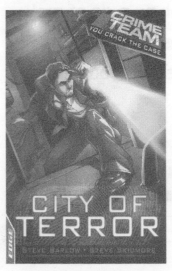

978 0 7496 9286 5 pb
978 1 4451 0845 2 eBook

978 0 7496 9285 8 pb
978 1 4451 0846 9 eBook